LENTIL SOUP

Carole Tremblay

illustrated by
Maurèen Poignonec

translated by
Charles Simard

ORCA BOOK PUBLISHERS

Published in Canada and the United States in 2021 by Orca Book Publishers.
orcabook.com

Library and Archives Canada Cataloguing in Publication
Title: Lentil soup / Carole Tremblay ; illustrated by Maurèen Poignonec ; translated by Charles Simard.
Other titles: Soupe aux lentilles. English
Names: Tremblay, Carole, 1959- author. | Poignonec, Maurèen, 1992- illustrator. |
Simard, Charles, 1983- translator.
Description: Translation of: La soupe aux lentilles.
Identifiers: Canadiana (print) 20210095520 | Canadiana (ebook) 20210095563 |
ISBN 9781459827011 (hardcover) | ISBN 9781459827028 (PDF) | ISBN 9781459827035 (EPUB)
Classification: LCC PS8589.R39428 S6813 2021 | DDC c843/.54—dc23

Library of Congress Control Number: 2020951464

Summary: A young mouse cleverly avoids eating his soup by distracting
his older brother with questions about every single ingredient.

Orca Book Publishers is committed to reducing the consumption of nonrenewable resources in
the making of our books. We make every effort to use materials that support a sustainable future.

Orca Book Publishers gratefully acknowledges the support for its publishing programs provided
by the following agencies: the Government of Canada, the Canada Council for the Arts and the
Province of British Columbia through the BC Arts Council and the Book Publishing Tax Credit.

We acknowledge the financial support of the Government of Canada through the National
Translation Program for Book Publishing, an initiative of the *Roadmap for Canada
Official Languages 2013-2018: Education, Immigration, Communities*, for our translation activities.

Cover and interior artwork by Maurèen Poignonec
Cover design by Ella Collier
Edited by Liz Kemp
Translated by Charles Simard

Printed and bound in China.

24 23 22 21 • 1 2 3 4

It's ready! Come eat!

1. UNCLE HERMAN MADE IT.

It's you and me, saucepan!

2. DAD BOUGHT IT AT THE SOUP SHOP. THAT'S A STORE WHERE THEY SELL SOUP AT THE PUMP.

I'll take a liter.

3. A FAIRY PUT IT IN THE FRIDGE LAST NIGHT.

Oh! The soup fairy passed by!

4. SOMEONE CAME TO THE DOOR TO SELL US SOME.

It's for my trip to the big city.

1. THEY'RE A KIND OF STONE YOU COLLECT AT AN OASIS IN THE MIDDLE OF THE DESERT.

2. THEY GROW IN PODS, LIKE GREEN PEAS, ON A PLANT THAT'S 30 CENTIMETERS HIGH.

3. THEY'RE BUTTONS THAT YOU PULL OFF THE BACKS OF TOADS.

4. THEY'RE LITTLE SHELLS THAT YOU FIND ON ROCKS AT THE SEASHORE. CRABS JUST LOVE THEM.

1. CARROTS GROW HIDDEN IN THE SOIL.

2. THEY'RE PICKED OFF THE FACES OF SNOWMEN AND THEN KEPT IN THE FRIDGE SO THEY DON'T LOSE THEIR FLAVOR.

3. THEY GROW ON TALL TREES KNOWN AS CARROTREES.

4. THEY'RE THE CLAWS OF A FIRE DRAGON.

1. IT'S A TYPE OF TREE THAT GROWS IN THE LAND OF ELVES.

2. IT'S MADE WITH DOUGH THAT'S A MIXTURE *OF CELL PHONES* AND *RICE*. THEN THEY ADD GRASS TO MAKE IT GREEN.

3. IT'S A PLANT THAT WAS DISCOVERED IN THE JUNGLE BY TWO PEOPLE NAMED HENRY AND CELINE.

4. THEY'RE THE STALKS OF A PLANT THAT GROWS IN A VEGETABLE GARDEN.

Onions grow in the earth. They have long green stems that are very straight. When you want to grow certain flowers, like tulips and hyacinths, you plant bulbs that are also called onions. But they aren't edible.

No, the tomato is the fruit of a small shrub called a tomato plant. There are several varieties. There are cherry tomatoes, which are very small, and beefsteak tomatoes, which are very, very big. The first tomatoes came from the Indigenous Peoples of South America.

1. IS SALT DRIED CROCODILE TEARS?

That'll be delicious on my chips!

2. SHINY, HARD SNOWFLAKES FROM THE SOUTH POLE?

One by one...

3. GRAINS OF SALTY SAND FROM THE SEASHORE?

Those come from sandcastles. Our very best.

Sea Salt

Okay, I'll explain, but afterward will you eat?

Yes!

Salt can come from two places.
You can collect it from salt marshes. They
are flat stretches of land along the shoreline,
where salty water settles. When the sun
evaporates the water, the salt that was in it
stays on the ground, and you can gather it.

1. IS IT GROUND-UP DRAGON SCALES?

2. IT'S A MIXTURE OF ASHES AND SPICY CHILIS?

3. IT'S WITCHES' HAIR TURNED TO POWDER?

Where do pots
come from?

LENTIL SOUP

When making this recipe, be sure
an adult is around to supervise.

INGREDIENTS:

1 tablespoon olive oil
1 onion, finely chopped
1 garlic clove, finely chopped
2 celery stalks, diced
2 large carrots, diced
1 can (3 ⅓ cups) diced or crushed tomatoes
4 cups broth (vegetable, chicken or beef)
1 teaspoon dried oregano
1 bay leaf
½ teaspoon dried basil
½ teaspoon thyme
½ teaspoon paprika
Salt and pepper to taste
1 cup dried lentils

DIRECTIONS:

1. Sauté the onion, garlic, celery and carrots
in the olive oil for 5 minutes.

2. Add the tomatoes, broth and spices.

3. Simmer for 15 minutes.

4. Add the lentils and let simmer for
an additional 30 minutes.

5. Remove the bay leaf before serving.

Carole Tremblay has been working in children's literature for almost 30 years in a variety of roles, such as bookseller, library assistant, literary critic, editor and author. She has written over 70 books for young readers and was the coauthor of the books adapted from the popular Toopy and Binoo series. Carole lives in Montreal.

Maurèen Poignonec studied fine arts in Versailles, Paris and Strasbourg. She was recognized for her work at the Angoulême International Comics Festival and has illustrated picture books and novels with several European publishing houses. Maurèen lives in France.